I0584768

EVEN SALT LOOKS LIKE SUGAR

a novella

YECHEILYAH YSRAYL

EVEN SALT LOOKS LIKE SUGAR Copyright © 2018 by Literary Korner Publishing. All rights reserved. Printed in the United States of America. No part of this book may be reproduced in any manner whatsoever without written permission except in the case of brief quotations embodied in critical articles and reviews.

EVEN SALT LOOKS LIKE SUGAR
Copyright © 2018 by Literary Korner Publishing.

This book is a work of fiction. Names, characters, businesses, organizations, places, events and incidents are the product of the author's imagination and are used fictitiously. Any resemblance to actual persons, living or dead, events, or locales is entirely coincidental and used fictitiously.

For information contact :
Yecheilyah Ysrayl
yecheilyah@yecheilyahysrayl.com
http://www.yecheilyahysrayl.com

First Edition : October, 2018

CHAPTER ONE

What was it about a little girl's screams that awakened the fight in her? It was the only time her own daydreams didn't block out the commotion going on down the street. Wanda blew a breath, her knees bent as she lay face-up on the cot and tapped her feet on the floor. No box springs. No bed rails. No headboard. Just a twin-sized bed in the middle of the floor. In the corner of the room, black garbage bags filled with her clothing fell clumsily, one on top of the other. And the fan blew hot air in from the window along with the sounds of arguing. But Wanda didn't hear a thing. Something was always going on in this house. It was why she'd mastered the art of tuning everything out. She didn't hear the noise unless she wanted to hear it. Miss Cassaundra called it creepy and got tired of calling her more than once. Wanda smiled despite herself. Miss Cassaundra was the woman she mostly wanted to tune out. Nonetheless, she didn't hear the noise flying into her window from whomever it was, doing whatever it was outside. Even when she stood up from her cot on the floor to stand by the open window, her arms folded, she heard nothing until the screams wafted through the openings of the fan and into her ears.

"Come on here, girl," said the voice.

Wanda lifted the window up higher and grabbed the handle on the white boxed-sized fan, lowering it to the floor. She took its place, sitting inside the crook of the windowsill, watching Anna Mae pull and yank her daughter's arm, propelling her to walk faster. The girl's tiny feet kicked up dust on the New Orleans road.

Every country town was the same. Acreage of land separated houses and trailers, the gas station or corner store, not seen for miles. It was too far to walk, though many did. Too many non-working cars parked too close together as children played in the middle of the road, running when the cars came. Either they ran to the side of the road, thick with trees and grassland, or onto the other side where the family trailers sat on cinderblocks. Horns honked as voices laughed and a relative scolded them.

"Get ya'll lil asses out the street."

Most likely, an uncle or cousin. Everyone either knew one another or was related in some way. Most of the families survived off the money they got for the land their trailers sat on. The oil companies profited off the ignorance of the poor. Ten thousand dollars a year sounded like a lot of money to people who have never had anything. That combined with Food Stamps and welfare could make some hood rich. Meanwhile, the oil companies raked in millions off the land as it sucked out all its nutrients and fed its owners pennies. St. Bernard Parish was no different. The first, third, and fifteenth of the month—because Miss Cassaundra got three checks—were like holidays. Fights were common, and everyone's business was in the street—literally.

"And don't come back," yelled the man to the woman's back. Anna Mae spun around, causing the girl to feel dizzy and fall at the sudden change of pace.

"You think I need this? I don't need you or ya raggedly...."

"Eh, watch yo mouth, girl!" yelled the man as Anna brushed the dirt off her daughter's clothing, talking as she did so.

"Don't you dare. Okay? Don't you dare."

"You heard what I said."

"So what? She ain't yours, no how. Come on here, girl," she said, grabbing the girl's hand again.

"Damn," whispered Wanda under her breath, fanning herself with her hand. *It's gonna be some good gossip about this later.*

The man stood back as if someone had thrown something heavy his way and it landed in the center of his chest like a gust of wind so strong it almost knocked him down. His lips turned up and his head tilted before he turned to walk away.

The little girl blinked and wiped the dirt from her hands as the walking began again. She was thankful for the break the fall created. Her little legs were tired, and she hoped for some rest. As mother and daughter walked on, the man charged up behind the two, and grabbed the woman by her hair.

"Oh shit," said Wanda, standing back from the windowsill as she watched.

"Mike! Mike, please!" screamed the woman.

It took the little girl a while to notice that the sound was coming from her mother. The man was now dragging her down the road by her hair.

"Mom!" the girl screamed. The commotion caused the neighbors to exit their homes and Wanda to rush from the window. The scream had awakened something in her. Something that would later save her life.

"You gonna stop playing games," said the man.

The little girl screamed as her body was being swept up into the air. It felt like she was flying.

"It's okay, baby girl. I got you now," said a voice and the girl's cries quieted. She wasn't flying. It was just a neighbor, running with her in her arms.

"Mama," she cried again.

"Shhh," the woman cooed as they made it to the house. She put the girl down in front of a big-boned, golden brown-skinned woman, sitting on the couch.

"Go ahead now. I got it. Make the call."

"Yes, Miss Cassaundra," said the woman, scurrying away as the girl cried.

Wanda had stopped running when she reached the front room. She watched as Lavenia came rushing into the house, baby girl in her arms, and watched as she put her down in front of Miss Cassaundra, sitting on the sofa as was her custom.

"It's alright now child. Everything gonna be alright," said Cassaundra, pushing the girl into Wanda's arms.

"Take her in the back, please. This fool out here making a scene again."

Wanda stared.

"Wanda!" called Cassaundra, jolting her from her daydream.

"Yea?"

"You heard what I said?"

Confusion washed over Wanda's face and Cassaundra frowned.

"Take her on in the back. I'm tired of repeating myself."

Wanda cut her eyes. She had hoped no one saw her standing there, so she could go back to her room. She adjusted her pink t-shirt and scratched at her hair before taking the girl's hand. Unlike the rest of the women in the house, Wanda was not half-naked.

"Come on, it's okay."

"Go on now, child. Ya safe now. Miss Wanda gonna take care of ya."

I am? Wanda sighed. *Here we go again. I watch the kids and she pockets the money.*

"I want my mama!" cried the girl.

Cassaundra rolled her eyes. *I'm too old for this shit.* "Ya mama be back soon. Now go on," she said.

Wanda held onto the girl's hand, and Cassaundra watched as the two walked down the hall. The double-wide trailer was long with extra rooms, and a back deck and front porch had been installed. Wanda and the little girl bypassed several half-dressed women coming in, through the kitchen from the backdoor, into the extra rooms Cassaundra had built specifically for her guests. Men followed closely behind the women, some holding onto their hands as they led them. Various conversations and laughter could be heard throughout the house.

"Lottie," called Cassaundra.

A tall, brown-skinned, older man, leaned against the wall. He had been silently watching the show and picking his teeth with a toothpick. He turned to face Cassaundra.

"Make me a drink," she said, leaning back into the sofa.

The man nodded like an obedient servant who questioned nothing and began walking down the hall. He bypassed Wanda and smacked her butt. She turned around quickly.

"What I tell you about yo nasty-ass hands!" she yelled, startling the girl.

"Lottie" called Cassaundra, "leave that girl alone and bring me my drink."

Wanda shook her head. *I can't wait to leave this house.*

CHAPTER TWO

The two weren't much different from each other, and in a strange way, they were almost the same person. Wanda looked down at the girl, her hand sweaty in hers as they walked down the crowded hall of the trailer home. The little girl was her ten years ago, when her father ran off with one of Cassaundra's hookers and never came back.

The two entered the empty room. On the floor next to the cot was a bottle with clear liquid inside, a hair clip, a toothbrush, toothpaste, a jar of water and a towel. Along the walls were black plastic bags as well as a fan on the floor that blew hot air. Wanda rushed to the window.

"It's hot as hell in this house," she whined as she put the fan back into the window. Not that it would help. It wasn't going to do anything but blow in hot air from the outside.

"When the air getting fixed?" asked Wanda, loud enough for anyone to hear. The central air was messed up again. *How somebody, who always getting paid, not have money to fix stuff?*

"Don't start that damn complaining in my house girl," said Cassaundra's voice. "Lottie! Bring me my drink."

Wanda shook her head.

"Go head, have a seat," she said pointing to the cot. But the little girl just stood with her head down.

"Or you can sit on the floor."

The girl's head jerked up, and she quickly took a seat on the cot. Wanda smirked.

"That's what I thought. Let's get you cleaned up. Wait here."

The girl grabbed Wanda's arm and the woman peeled her fingers away. "It's okay. I'm coming back."

Reluctantly, the girl let go and Wanda walked over to one of the black garbage bags. She turned it upside down and emptied the clothing onto the floor.

"We gonna find you something real nice," she said as she continued to look through the clothing. She pulled out a pink and white dress and smiled. Wanda stood and walked back over to the cot.

"This gonna look real pretty on you," she said as tears escaped the little girl's eyes.

"Oh no, don't cry. Ya mama be back soon. *That was a lie. Daddy never came back.* But she couldn't say that to a little girl.

"Hey, what's your name?"

The girl's big brown eyes stared.

"Come on," said Wanda, hitting the girl playfully.

"Abby," said her shaky voice.

"Nice to meet you Abby. I'm Wanda. You know, that's a very pretty name. And I got a very pretty dress to go along with it."

Abby smiled.

"There you go. You wanna stand up for me? Let's get you outta these clothes."

Abby stood. And Wanda lifted the girl's shirt over her head and helped her into the dress.

"You know," she said, helping Abby to put her arms into the dress. "You're not the only one. Miss Cassaundra always taking folks in. She thinks it's some kinda calling. But then again, Miss Cassaundra is some kinda liar. I know you young and all. But that's just something you gotta know up front. She got tricks all up her sleeves."

Abby just stared as Wanda pulled the dress down over her body.

"Anyway, you ain't the first. I remember my first time here. It's scary at first. But you get used to it. Just stay outta Lottie's way, okay?"

The little girl stared as Wanda reached for a small rag at the edge of the bed, picked up the bottle of water and poured some of the water on the rag. She reached out for the girl who pushed it away.

"Hey…hey…whoa…. Stop it."

Abby fought the towel. But Wanda pinned her arms down on the bed.

"Hey. I said stop. Now I know you don't like it. But you ain't got much of a choice. Got it?"

Tears welled in the corners of the girl's eyes.

"Are you calm?"

Abby didn't answer.

"Are you calm?" Wanda repeated.

Abby shook her head. Wanda let her go and reached for the bottle of water again.

"I know it ain't perfect. But it's clean." Wanda drenched the towel in the liquid and wrung it out on the floor.

"We'll clean that up later. Got a big towel in the bag," she said, wiping at Abby's face.

"Maybe we ain't in the best of situations. But I'm clean. Ya here?"

The girl blinked.

"I don't smoke, I don't drink, and I don't get high. I don't play that shit. It's why I got my own room. Got it?"

Abby continued to stare as Wanda wiped her face, arms, and legs.

"Lucky ya lil butt in here with me. Give me that other arm. You hungry?"

Abby stared.

"You gonna have to start talking now. We don't read minds around here. Wait here."

Wanda exited the room and Abby sat like a statue on the stained, uncovered cot. She looked around at the large black bags and knew they would look like monsters in the dark. But mama wasn't here to turn on the nightlight. There was no nightlight. She sat frozen on the bed, blocking out the sounds of the people in the hall and wondered when mama was coming back. *The lady said she be back soon.* The thought filled her with hope and she played with the ruffles on the pink and white dress.

CHAPTER THREE

Wanda puckered her lips as she danced in the mirror that leaned against the wall, and laughed, cutting her eyes at Abby, sitting on the cot.

"Okay. Let's hear it. I got ten minutes to spare. Run it down."

Abby rolled her eyes. *Not this again.*

"Now. I ain't got all day."

Abby sighed. "Two times one equals two. Two times two equals four. Two times three equals six. Two times four equals…"

Abby paused. "I gotta do all my times tables?"

Wanda examined the room as she turned to face the girl sitting on the cot. At least she'd managed to get her off the floor, the past few weeks. The bed set already made it look normal. Well, it wasn't exactly a *set*. More like a box spring on rails and a little dresser. But that was better than nothing. Her own clothes were still in black plastic bags, stacked one on top the other, in the closet.

"Yes. Every single one. You ain't about to be like these stupid little girls out here."

Abby laughed as Wanda took a seat beside her on the cot.

"I'm serious. Now, you listen here. I don't want you out in these streets. You may not have a mama. But you smart. You can do anything you want."

Abby grew sad at the thought of her mother. It'd been at least a month and there was no sign of her. She looked down at her feet. Wanda must have had a good night because she bought her new shoes and a new dress. And she couldn't wait to show it off to her friends. Wanda was her mother now, she had already decided in her head. At least, she would pretend she was until her mother returned. This is how she coped. Abby jumped from the bed.

"Can I go now?"

Wanda turned up her lip. "You think you slick, don't you?"

Abby laughed. "What?"

"What nothing. Go 'head. But tomorrow, I wanna hear threes and fours."

"Ah man," whined Abby, slumping her shoulders on her way out the room.

Wanda smiled and shook her head. *That girl.*

The woman stood and admired herself once more in the mirror leaning against the wall. It was more like one large vertical piece of glass someone found in an abandoned trailer.

She held onto her stomach, filled with butterflies and possibilities. Her interview was in two hours, and she hoped she'd get it this time. Maybe then, she'll be able to give Abby something more than a pair of shoes and a cheap dress. If she played her cards right, that girl would be her ticket out of here.

"Wanda!"

Wanda rolled her eyes. Years of hearing that voice got on her last nerve.

"What?"

"Don't *what* me," yelled Cassaundra from the hall. "Come here."

Wanda sighed and exited the room. The house was crowded as usual. Half-naked women paraded back and forth. Men walked in and out of rooms. And children ran back and forth from the kitchen to the back door. Wanda's heart dropped as she saw new faces. More orphans meant more money for Miss Cassaundra from the state.

"Yea?"

Cassaundra was lying on the couch as usual, a glass of whiskey in one hand and a cigarette in the other. The woman had a round face and was extremely beautiful and extremely overweight. She wore a head wrap on her head and a long red silk gown, down to her ankles, that covered her large body. She struggled to lean over while lying down, choosing to sit the glass down on the floor above her head but held onto the cigarette like it was hope itself. Once her drink and smoke were safe, the woman struggled to sit up as she held out her arm. This was Wanda's cue. Wanda held onto the woman's arm and pulled as she sat up. Once sitting up, Cassaundra put her feet into her silky red slippers. But they could only go halfway in. Her feet were too fat.

"Hand me my drink," she said, pointing to the floor.

Wanda frowned. *Why you put it down there, if you were just gonna want it again?* Cassaundra frowned back and gave the young woman a stern stare. And Wanda's shoulders slumped as she bent down and gave the woman her drink. Cassaundra winked and smiled at Lottie from across the room. He'd better appreciate her giving him a sneak peek. She didn't do nothing for free. Cassaundra stopped smiling and turned her attention back to Wanda, looking her up and down as Wanda gave her the glass.

"You going somewhere today?"

Wanda's heart skipped a beat as her stomach dropped. She

wasn't in the mood for Miss Cassaundra's foolishness. What she didn't know wouldn't hurt her.

"Got some errands to run. Why? What's up?"

Cassaundra inhaled the cigarette and blew the smoke into the air.

"What you dress so fancy for, then?"

Wanda frowned. "What? Nothing. Like I said, I got errands to run. What's up?"

"Don't sass talk me, girl. I ain't ya mammy."

"I'm not being smart. I'm just saying. I'm not going anywhere special."

"Good. We cleaning house. Got some social services people coming over today. Need you to gone and take Abby, Chris, and Nikki on downtown and get some clothes. And get somebody to comb them nappy heads of theirs too. I'll give you the money."

"What time they gonna be here?"

Cassaundra took a sip of her whiskey before answering.

"Couple hours."

Wanda's shoulders dropped. Her interview was in two hours.

"I can't."

Cassaundra paused and stared at the young woman in front of her.

"Hell you mean, you can't?"

"I told you. I got errands to run."

"Well, yo errands gonna have to wait."

Tears welled in the corners of Wanda's eyes. But she held them back.

"Miss Cassaundra, I can't."

"Your errands gonna have to wait, goddammit!" yelled

Cassaundra. Lottie laughed in the background.

"Ain't nothing more important than what we got going on here. You forget where you come from?"

Wanda looked away, holding on tight to the lump in her throat.

"Don't forget who took you in, lil heifa. Ain't seen ya no good daddy since he ran off. Remember that shit? I ain't the bad guy."

Wouldn't have met her, if this place didn't exist, thought Wanda.

"Are we done?"

Cassaundra looked Wanda up and down.

"Yea. We done. Don't be biting the damn hand that feed ya. Gone and get them chiren ready. Wasting all my damn time."

Wanda turned around and headed toward the back door to find the children who were playing behind the trailer.

"Abby! Chris! Nikki!" she yelled from the screen door, wiping the tears from her face as they fell. She would have to miss another interview.

CHAPTER FOUR

The social services people never came. They waited hours, jumping at the sound of every car engine grunting down the road and running to the door at every knock. But it was just Cassaundra's customers. Hours turned into more hours until the sun began to descend the sky, painting the city burnt orange and reddish. It was a trick. A joke. Wanda was sure of it. Cassaundra knew about her interview. She had to know. But who would snitch? Did Lottie rat her out? No. Lottie didn't know. She wouldn't give him the satisfaction of being in her business.

Wanda sprang from the cot and walked to the bedroom door, opened it, and looked down the hall.

"Abby. Abby come here."

The little girl pranced over. And Wanda shut the door.

"Did you tell Miss Cassaundra about my interview?"

"No!" yelled Abby.

"Calm down. I'm just asking. You remember what we talked about, right? About not trusting Miss Cassaundra?"

"Yea, I remember. I didn't say nothing. I promise."

Wanda bit her lip. Abby was telling the truth. So, who snitched? Wanda thought about the day she found out she had the interview. She was leaving her friend Rosa Lee's house, whose phone she'd used when she ran into Lavenia.

"What's got you so happy?" said the dark-skinned, toothless woman. She was smoking a cigarette. But Lavenia was on that stuff and it had made her skin darken and cling to her bones. A lot of their neighbors was like this. They nodded, bowing low enough

to be inches from the floor before jerking back again, brushing away bugs, only they could see as they unnecessarily cleaned, picking imaginary lint from their clothing, and laughing at jokes only they were in on—the real walking dead. Their skeletal bodies roamed the country roads early mornings, afternoons and late at night. Or they stood next to gas stations waiting for customers to come out, so they could collect change, their long skinny fingers curled into tight fists around the crack they sold their souls for.

Wanda cringed on the inside. Seeing her people like this made her physically sick. Lavenia was once pretty.

"It's a good day. That's all."

Lavenia frowned and inhaled the cigarette like it was the last one she would ever smoke.

"Hmm. Yea. How Abby doing?"

Diversion. Lavenia never asked about Abby. Lavenia only cared about one thing. Getting high. Wanda frowned at the thought. She was so excited, she hadn't noticed the signs.

"Oh, Abby is doing good, Miss Lavenia. I think she's adjusting real nice. You seen her mama any?"

Lavenia let the cigarette breathe some, exhaling smoke into the air before sucking on it again.

"Naw. Ain't seen her since that day."

She was talking about the day she carried Abby into Cassaundra's prison. Lavenia eyed the young lady in front of her. She had a shape like that once.

"You got some money? Let me borrow a couple dollars till my paycheck hit."

"I'm sorry Miss L. I ain't got nothing on me."

"I can walk with you to the house. All I need is a lil change."

"I can't. I'm broke."

Lavenia frowned. "You ain't no damn broke."

"Miss L. I am. For real. You know if I had it, you'd have it. I gotta get going. Tell Brandon I said hey."

Lavenia walked off in a hurry. Brandon was her son. She'd probably left him in the house by himself again.

Wanda bit her lip at her thoughts. Lavenia could have gotten mad at her for not giving her any money.

"Okay Abby. I believe you. Gone and finish playing. I gotta make a run."

Wanda grabbed her keys and headed for the door. She walked out the back, so she wouldn't have to pass Miss Cassaundra on the couch. She needed to test her theory that Lavenia ratted her out.

Wanda walked across the plush green grass of Cassaundra's ten acres and darted across the street to avoid walking in the front of the house. It was an unnecessary turn-around but worth not having to answer all fifty of Cassaundra's questions. As she walked, she noticed it was an unusually quiet evening. But then again, it was always like that when everybody thinks the people coming over. Every house is clean. And every child is bathed, wearing new clothes, full and happy. Wanda remembered when she was little. She loved it when *the people* came to inspect. That's what everybody called them, "the people." News of the social worker ladies coming to inspect the houses of the foster parents would spread throughout the community like wildfire.

"The people coming today," the neighbors would say, on

their way inside their houses to clean up. Then Miss Cassaundra would have someone to gather her and her friends and treat them like children were supposed to be treated. *Like Abby and her friends are being treated right now. Like the princesses they are.* Wanda smiled as she approached Rosa Lee's trailer, remembering when they were both small children, abandoned by their parents and raised by Miss Marie and Miss Cassaundra.

Wanda's father John, and his obsessive visits to Miss Cassaundra's, led to an argument with Wanda's mother Toni. That led to a 911 call from Miss Cassaundra, who was always watching and waiting for an opportunity to snitch. Toni received an unexpected visit from Child Protective Services. The caseworker asked if she used drugs, and Toni truthfully responded that she smoked marijuana, from time to time. According to John, who related the story to Wanda, that admission led to a child neglect proceeding against her in which the state claimed Toni did not properly care for her child. The only evidence presented on the petition was Toni's admission that she smoked marijuana. The court adjudicated her as "neglectful" and implemented a "family service plan," a combination of on-going state surveillance and mandatory "services." This led to John getting permanent custody of his daughter, until abandoning her at the Williams' house to run off with the woman he loved. Neither Toni nor John had been heard from since. And Wanda was raised by Miss Cassaundra Williams.

The mass removal of black children from their families, in ways, parallels the U.S. criminal legal system's mass removal of black men and women from their communities. The child welfare system claims to be a non-adversarial legal system dedicated to ensuring the well-being and safety of children. This claim obscures the oppressive political role it plays in monitoring, regulating, and punishing poor families. Every day in family court buildings across the country, thousands of people, but disproportionately black mothers, stand before child welfare officials and family court judges who subject their parenthood to extraordinary scrutiny and vilification. These judges and officials use consequences of poverty, such as several siblings sharing a single room or lack of adequate heat, as evidence of child neglect.

Rosa had a similar story, except her father was dead and she was taken from her mother due to neglect. Rosa's mom was like Lavenia. She got high. One day while hanging with some friends, she was sent up the road to cop. While Rosa's mother was gone, someone called "the people." When she returned, two white women were taking her daughter and her "friends" were gone.

Wanda and Rosa grew up in the system together and became best friends, like sisters. When the people were coming, they asked for extra stuff, and Cassaundra and Marie, Rosa's foster mother, would give them anything they wanted. The girls knew that if their guardians didn't give them what they wanted, they risked being discovered as unfit. And they could get all their children taken away and their money taken away.

"Hey girl," said Rosa, sitting on the porch of her single-wide trailer. At least Miss Marie had some decency. When Rosa had her own kids, she let her have her own spot on her land. Miss Cassaundra would never do that.

"Hey. You seen Miss L around here?" asked Wanda. Even though Lavenia was on drugs, Wanda had been taught to give those older than her respect, regardless of their situation. Miss

Cassaundra had done *something* right, at least.

"Lavenia? Why you looking for crackheads. What's wrong?"

Wanda waved a hand, laughing. "Naw, ain't nothing like that," she said, sitting down next to Rosa. "Missed my interview."

"How you do that?" asked Rosa.

"I think Lavenia snitched."

"Lavenia?" Rosa laughed. "Girl bye. Lavenia don't tell on nobody."

"Then who could it have been then? Only other people knew is me, you, and Abby. And I already grilled Abby."

"I don't know. You know how lil kids are. Can't really tell if they being truthful or not."

"No. I know when Abby lying. She wasn't. Unless yo ass told."

Rosa leaned back, her light skin darkening under the shadow of the sun. It would be pitch black soon. In Louisiana, if the street lights weren't on, or if the moon didn't light your path, you wouldn't be able to see in front of you. It got that dark.

"Now you know I ain't no damn snitch, Bitch."

Wanda laughed loudly. "Why you gotta call me out my name for?"

"Cause I can't believe you'll say some shit like that."

Wanda waved. "Calm down, girl. I'm just messing. I don't know what Imma do though Rose. How Imma get away from the Wicked Witch of the West, if these nosey-ass people keep telling her my business?"

Rosa smiled. *The Wizard of Oz* had been their favorite childhood movie to watch together. They would watch it repeatedly and fantasize about going back to Kansas, away from the world of their evil foster mothers. They were both Dorothy.

And Miss Cassaundra and Miss Marie were both wicked witches. At twenty-years-old, Rosa was four years older than Wanda and had been freed from her witch when she was pregnant with her fourth child. Miss Marie didn't want to deal with more children on top of the foster children she already had. And between the food stamps and welfare checks she got for the kids, Rosa could pay her bills without working. Rosa had gotten lucky, but she still felt sorry for her friend.

"You'll figure something out. You know you can stay here with me."

"And where yo five kids gonna sleep?" asked Wanda.

"On the floor, shit," said Rosa, dragging the word out.

"You know you ain't putting them kids on no floor. Social services would have you *under* the jail."

Rosa's lip twisted. "Humph. I shole the hell will. They be aiight."

Wanda laughed. "You crazy, girl."

"You reschedule your interview, right?" asked Rosa.

"No, not yet."

"Why? Girl, you better get on it. My cousins 'nem be getting appointments after appointments. You know you can reschedule them shits."

"Why you curse so much?" asked Wanda.

"Cause I'm a cursing ass, that's why."

Wanda laughed. "What Imma do with you?" The friends laughed some more as the sun disappeared and the sky turned black.

CHAPTER FIVE

So, Miss Lavenia didn't do it.

Wanda bit her lip and bounced her leg up and down as she looked around the room. A large desk was in front of her and plaques lined the walls. She wiggled in the cushioned office chair. The issue still bothered her.

"Ms. Tate?"

Wanda jerked up and cleared away her thoughts as the short brown-skinned woman walked into the room. She had been waiting for someone to hear her case at the aid office for about twenty minutes. *It's about time someone showed up.* Wanda stood.

"Yes, that's me," she said, shaking the woman's free hand. The woman's other hand was occupied with an envelope. Wanda wondered what was in her files. *Focus girl. You can't afford to daydream today.*

The woman smiled.

"Nice to meet you Ms. Tate. I'm Mrs. Clark."

Wanda sat back down as Mrs. Clark sat behind the desk, in an expensive-looking office chair. She removed papers from the envelop and swiveled around in her seat, while glancing at the papers and holding a pen in her hand, the kind of thing professionals do to look important. *That chair could buy Abby a whole trunk of clothes.*

"Okay. So we reviewed your case. And all you have to do is, bring us proof of residency and both your social security cards and birth certificates, and we can get you in."

Wanda's heart beat fast. Rosa had told her about how she could get an apartment at one of the low-income apartment houses and work in the office of the building to help with bills. She didn't think it was possible. But then again, Rosa had family members who knew how to get blood from a turnip when it came to getting money from the government. And Rosa was a pro. There was only one problem: only single black mothers could qualify for the special program. It's how Rosa got her trailer.

Mrs. Clark saw the look of concern on Wanda's face. She stopped swiveling, put the papers down on her desk, and lowered her voice.

"Look, people do it all the time. Little brothers, little sisters, cousins, any young family member they may want to live with them. She doesn't have to be *your* daughter. If you can prove that you have custody of her, that you're her legal guardian, I can get you in."

Okay, thought Wanda. *Two problems.* Miss Cassaundra has everyone's paperwork, including hers. Even though Wanda took care of Abby, Miss Cassaundra was her guardian.

"Think you can get that to me by tomorrow?"

Mrs. Clark's words jolted Wanda out of her thoughts.

"By tomorrow?"

Mrs. Clark shook her head.

"Can you give me till Friday?" *That will buy me at least three days.*

"We have a small window here, Miss Tate."

"Yes, I know. I just need more time."

"I can give you until Thursday. But that's the best I can do. These positions are exclusive and go very, very fast."

Shit. Just two days. "Yes. I understand," said Wanda, standing, smoothing out the wrinkles in her one good pantsuit. It was the only one she had, and she used it for every interview. It got to the point that the whole neighborhood could tell where she was going with it on. Mrs. Clark stood.

"Remember, there are actual mothers applying for this position. Ms. Flowers is a very good friend of mine, so I'm going out on a limb here because of her recommendation."

So, shall I bow and kiss your precious ring? Ms. Flowers was the old lady everyone hated at the office. The woman was bitter because she had to sort through everyone's case and make recommendations. She hated the women because she hated her job.

"You have to get this paperwork to me," continued Mrs. Clark.

Yea, yea. Whatever. "I'll have it to you by Thursday," Wanda said. "You got my word."

Mrs. Clark smiled. "That's what I wanna hear. I'm so proud of you. Good luck!"

Proud of me? You don't even know me, lady.

Wanda fake smiled back and walked out of the office, down the hall, down the flights of stairs, and out of the federal building.

There was no way Miss Cassaundra was going to part with those papers. And Wanda had no idea how she was going to get them.

CHAPTER SIX

Wanda dragged her body through the front door.

"Wanda!" yelled Abby, running into her arms.

Miss Cassaundra was sitting up on the sofa, as usual. The television replayed an episode of *One Life to Live*. Wanda stared absentmindedly at the television screen. *I only have one life to live all right, and it's not going to be in this house.* She cut her eyes at Cassaundra, her foot dangling off the couch. Wanda frowned and turned her attention to Abby.

"Hey. You been good today?"

"Hell naw," interrupted Cassaundra.

"Yes, I was!" whined Abby. Wanda ignored Cassaundra and took the girl's hand.

"Come on, I got something for you."

"Oh, so you just gonna walk yo lil ass pass me and not speak?"

"Hey Miss Cassaundra," murmured Wanda.

"How it go today?" asked Cassaundra.

Damn she nosey. She knows she don't care how it went. Just trying to be in somebody business.

"It went good. I need my social security card from you though." *I need Abby's too. But let's just see if I'll get mine.*

"Hell you need that for? What sneaky shit you got planned?"

"Never mind."

Cassaundra grunted and took out a new cigarette as Wanda and Abby walked to the back. Wanda opened her bedroom door and froze.

"What are you doing in my room?"

Lottie sat up on the cot and took a sip from a plastic cup. *Way too early for him to be drinking.* Wanda's blood boiled as she tried not to lose it in front of Abby.

"I asked you a question."

Lottie stood and grinned. "You ain't gonna get it. She ain't gonna give it to you."

Wanda felt the rage burn her throat. It wasn't like he was telling her something she didn't already know.

"Get out. Get out of my room before I call Miss Cassaundra. You know you not allowed in my room."

Lottie walked up to Wanda. His lips brushed past her ear on his way out of the room.

"You ain't gonna get it, cause she ain't got it."

He let the words hang in the air, knowing they left her desperate for more. Wanda released Abby's hand and spun around as Lottie walked down the hall. He turned around and his eyes locked with hers. *What do you know?* Her eyes begged. Why was hope such a fleeting thing? Giving little doses at a time, being stingy with information? Lottie smirked, turned back around, walked down the hall, and out the back door.

***

"You think he lying?"

Rosa and Wanda walked along the dirt road, with Rosa's five children, aged ten and under, in tow. They were on their way to the store up the road to get the kids some snacks. It was the third which meant Rosa got her check.

"Ya'll come on here now!" yelled Rosa behind her. "In front of me, come on."

The children bounced and skipped along, eager to see what they would pick out next at the store. Wanda smiled at Rosa's three-year-old, the youngest boy. His little legs worked over-time to catch up to the other children. Rosa's womb had been blessed. Three, five, six, eight, and ten. Boy, girl, girl, boy, girl. Wanda still remembered when she was pregnant with the oldest.

"I dunno girl. He is close as hell with Cassaundra. He probably know where it is. Maybe Cassaundra ain't the person who got it. Maybe he do."

Wanda bit her lip. It was possible. But she wasn't asking Lottie for nothing.

"Lottie, ole perverted self. I ain't asking him for nothing."

"Egypt! What I say? Get yo ass in front of us," Rosa shook her head. "Girl these kids be driving me crazy, acting brand new."

Wanda laughed.

"Know they don't walk behind me like that. I don't know what I would do something happen to my kids. Walk in front of me. How many times Imma say it?"

Wanda looked down at the dirt road and smiled. Rosa could go from talking to you and then talking to her children, with no break in-between. She waited until she got them together before speaking again. The lights from the H&H store came into view and the women walked in silence as the children picked up pace, excited to see light at the end of the tunnel. The only store close enough to walk, without fainting from the Southern heat, was two miles away. And neither Wanda or Rosa had a car. They entered the coolness of the store, the crisp, dry air hitting them on the way in.

"It smell cold in here," Alice, Rosa's oldest, said.

"How it *smell* cold? Girl say stuff that make sense."

Wanda laughed as she scanned the chip aisle.

"Now gone and get something. And get outta grown-folk business. Shoot." The children ran off and Rosa joined Wanda.

"I know you ain't feeling it, but he may be yo only way out," Rosa said, picking up a giant bag of *Flamin Hots*. Rosa loved hot stuff and could eat the whole bag by herself. She opened it and popped a few Cheetos into her mouth. Wanda shook her head. Rosa ate food from the store before she paid all the time. She ate chips, drank soda, chewed gum. She never walked out without paying though. Plus, the Arabs knew she got money for her kids, so they didn't mind. They knew when the Rosa Five came through, they were about to get paid.

"You know they only gave me two days."

"Two days?" asked Rosa, chewing.

"Yea. I got till Thursday to provide paperwork proving I got custody of Abby."

"But you don't have custody of Abby," Rosa said, shaking her head.

"Exactly. I will in two days though. Somehow."

"Damn, I need a drink. Hold on. Chris. Chris!"

"Yes mama?"

"Bring me a coke."

"Why do you eat in the store?" laughed Wanda.

"Girl, they know me," said Rosa laughing. "Chris hurry up! Thirsty as hell."

The chubby, smooth-skinned eight-year-old was adorable. Wanda smiled as he handed his mother a can of coke and wobbled off. Rosa opened the can and gulped it down, washing the chips down her throat. "Damn, that's good."

"I don't see how you do that," said Wanda.

"Do what?"

"Drink soda after eating something hot. My throat would be burning like hell."

"First, it's not *soda,* it's pop," said Rosa. "And second, I'm used to it."

"Yo booty gonna be burning when you boo-boo. I don't see how yo throat ain't burning now," laughed Wanda, watching Rosa empty the can.

"I don't know what Imma do," she continued, deciding on a bag of *Cheese Lay's.*

"You gonna have to give him some," said Rosa.

Wanda paused. "What? Girl, what I look like? One of Cassaundra's hoes?"

"Okay. Well tease him or something. Get on his good side. Find out what he knows. You know he know where she hiding yo stuff. Kids! Come on, let's roll."

Wanda threw the bag of chips back on the shelf. Suddenly, she felt like she would puke at the thought of eating anything.

CHAPTER SEVEN

Wanda admired herself in the mirror again for the tenth time. She hated the make-up caked on top of her smooth brown skin. She'd never been much of the make-up type. With no mother, no one had ever taught her how to apply it. And she wasn't going to rely on YouTube. Wanda turned to the side and sighed. *Told that girl this dress was too tight.*

Rosa had volunteered to keep Abby for the night, so Wanda could take care of her business. It was the only place Miss Cassaundra would allow Abby to go without getting suspicious. Everyone knew how close Wanda and Rosa were since they'd grown up together. And everyone knew how much Rosa loved her children. "I'll just say I'm having a sleepover for Egypt or something," Rosa had said, on their way back to the house. Wanda had invited Lottie to her room, through one of the other women. Now she wished she'd taken it back.

"I knew you would come around."

Wanda jumped at the sound of Lottie's voice and cringed on the inside. Lottie was in his early forties, brown-skinned, with a low-cut fade and a nappy beard he kept picking at. But hard living made him look older. He was a thin man, tall and could always be found chewing on a toothpick, smoking a cigarette, or drinking from plastic cups. *No wonder he so skinny*, thought Wanda. She rarely saw the man eat. He had been with Cassaundra for years and everyone thought secretly, he was her hit man. *How could one woman put that kind of fear in people when she was too fat to move?* Lottie cleared his throat, startling Wanda out of her thoughts. He walked into the room and closed the door. Wanda swallowed hard and tried to smile. Lottie leaned against the wall.

"Cut the crap Wanda. We both know yo stuck-up ass ain't tryna give it up. So what you want?"

"What you said yesterday. You know something. I wanna know what you know," Wanda said, pulling her dress down some more. As much as she wanted to sit, she'd just be giving Lottie a sneak peek. *Dammit Rosa. This tight-ass dress.*

"Got in yo head the other day, huh?"

"Yea, whatever. If Cassaundra ain't got my stuff, then who does? I know you know where she hiding it."

"Actually, I don't. But I know who is."

Wanda let her arm fall to her side. "Okay. And? Who? Stop playing games, Lottie. My life is on the line."

"First, I don't give a damn about yo life. And secondly, you should be glad I'm even helping yo ass. I could not say shit. Or, I could tell Cassaundra about that fancy lil job you got."

Wanda folded her arms. "I don't have a job."

Lottie laughed. "You still don't get it do you? We got eyes all around this bitch. I know everything about you, girl."

"So, *you* snitched."

"No. But Ms. Flowers hate yo ass. Ain't take much convincing to give you up."

That bitch, thought Wanda.

"Is that where you was at yesterday? Yo lil fancy job? Better not let Cassaundra find out."

"First, I only get the job if I can get the paperwork. So yo *eyes* don't know shit."

"Anyway, like I said. I don't know where it's at. I can't help you." Lottie turned away and opened the bedroom door.

"But you said you know who," Wanda said, before Lottie walked all the way out of the room. She knew she sounded desperate but what choice did she have?

Lottie turned around. The two stared for a second.

"John got it," he said.

Wanda froze as her heart beat so close to her chest that she thought Lottie could hear it.

"How do you know my father?"

Lottie shrugged. Wanda backed up to the wall. The emotion grew inside her throat as it tried to force its way up.

"Has...has he had it this whole time?"

Lottie shrugged again as if she was asking about a missing hairpiece. "Pretty much."

"This means..." Wanda slid onto the floor, not caring if her panties were showing or not. The tears had found their way to the corners of her eyes.

"Get out," she said.

Lottie smirked and walked out the door. Getting rid of him was too easy. He did this. He meant to do this. He wanted to hurt her. Wanda let the tears go and crawled over to the cot, crying into the mattress. It was a nightmare she couldn't wake up from. If her father had her paperwork the entire time, it meant Miss Cassaundra didn't have legal custody of her. It meant she'd been a willing prisoner the entire time. She could have left whenever she wanted to.

CHAPTER EIGHT

"Forget it," said Wanda, sitting up on the cot. The sky was black. She'd cried herself to sleep. She had wasted half a day messing with Lottie. Slipping into some sneakers, she avoided the mirror as she stood. She knew she looked a mess. Her dress was too tight and too short. Her hair was disheveled from sleeping for hours, her eyes red and puffy and her cheeks stained with the streaks of tears. Wanda didn't want to look at herself. She knew she looked just how she felt. *Like crap*. Instead, she marched out of the room.

As usual, Miss Cassaundra was sitting on the couch in the living room, watching TV. She turned to see Wanda storming down the hallway.

"What you and Lottie into it for now?"

"You lied to me!" yelled Wanda.

"Whoa. I think you need to calm yo lil ass down."

"No. No more," said Wanda. Tears gushed from her eyes and her hands shook.

Cassaundra looked the young woman up and down.

"You going out tonight?" she said, smirking as she lifted a pack of cigarettes."

"You smoke too much," said Wanda.

Cassaundra took a single cigarette out of the pack, put it between her lips, grabbed a lighter and used her other hand to hide the flame from the air as she lit the cigarette. She put the lighter back down on the sofa, inhaled thankfully and blew smoke out into the air.

"What business is it of yours?"

Wanda shook her head. The conversation was fruitless.

"Are you my *legal* guardian?"

Cassaundra froze and the cigarette dangled between her lips. She put it out in the ashtray next to her. It had suddenly lost its flavor.

"Don't ask questions you don't want the answers to."
Tears fell freely from Wanda's eyes.

"Tell me the truth."

"Gone back in your room, little girl," waved Cassaundra.

"Tell me the truth!"

"You can't handle the truth, goddammit!" yelled Cassaundra. "Ya no good mammy and ya no good daddy left you. That's the truth. Left you here like a dog."

Wanda folded her arms. *That's a lie.*

"Tell me… Tell me I wasn't your prisoner. Tell me…" Wanda choked on her words. For the first time, she saw a glint of mercy in Cassaundra's eyes and decided to take advantage of it. "Please. You've taken everything from me. Please, just tell me the truth. You owe me that much."

"I don't owe you shit."

Cassaundra avoided eye contact with Wanda and stared straight ahead at the television. Seconds passed between them. But to Wanda, it seemed too long. Cassaundra picked her cigarette back up, put it to her lips, and lit it again. She inhaled, letting the nicotine savor in her throat and calm her nerves. She took two more puffs before speaking again.

"John was a good man," she began. "But he had a problem." Cassaundra pointed to Wanda before turning back toward the television. "Couldn't leave the pipe alone."

Wanda's heart swelled as surprise crept into her eyes. *Pipe?* When Cassaundra turned to face Wanda, she saw the look on her face.

"Yea that's right. Ya daddy was a junkie. Hell, my girls is good," she said, chuckling, but not like a real laugh. "But coochie ain't never had a nigga strung out like that. I knew it. Everybody knew it. Whole damn neighborhood knew it."

I didn't know it. Wanda's heart sank as a wave of hot air of embarrassment for her father, came over her.

"I may not be the most perfect person in the world, okay? But I don't allow that kinda mess to go on in my house and with my girls. You wanna smoke crack, you can do it out there," she said, pointing to the door. "So, he had to go."

"You put my father out?"

"I put a junkie out!" yelled Cassaundra. "I sure in the fuck did. What else you wanna know? Huh?"

Wanda sat on the floor, next to the couch and faced the television, frozen with shock as Cassaundra spoke.

"So yes, I took you in, just like I took all these other chiren running around here in. Just like I took that damn Abby you love so much in. When ya daddy left, you stayed. It's as simple as that. Black folk don't go around adopting kids and signing papers and *legalizing* shit. Thought you was smart. You should know that by now. We see something that need to be done, and we handle it. I let you stay here, put food in your stomach and clothes on ya back. I did that. I handled it. You think I do this shit for my health?"

Tears began to creep up into Cassaundra's throat and she fake coughed to clear it away. But Wanda still heard it in her voice.

"What? Ya'll don't think I get tired of sitting on this damn couch? Can't move around a lot. Can't see my fucking feet? I ain't have the luxury of having people to take care of me. I ain't got no fucking family. So guess what? I made my own." A tear escaped and she wiped it away quickly. "This is my house. My house!" Cassaundra's voice shook the floor beneath her. "And I do whatever I want to, in my house. I kick out junkies, and I raise children don't nobody else want."

A pain hit Wanda in her chest. *Is that what happened? Did no one want me?* It was a blow Cassaundra meant to hit. She was hurting, and she wanted to hurt someone else.

"No, I ain't ya damn *legal* guardian and I ain't got no papers. But I took care of ya. I did that."

Tears continued to fall from Wanda's eyes.

"No. You imprisoned me. Made me think I couldn't leave."

"I never said that. You made that up in ya own mind."

"No!" yelled Wanda, standing. "Stop doing that. Stop lying to yourself. Stop playing the victim. You could have told me. When I was older. You could have given me a choice."

Wanda was surprised to not hear a comeback. She kept going while she still could.

"You are miserable and I'm sorry. I'm sorry you let your weight control your life. And I'm sorry you feel like you have no one."

Another tear escaped Cassaundra's eye. She didn't wipe it

away that time. Wanda continued.

"So, you surround yourself with people. That's why there are so many people in this house, all the time. That's why you take in so many children. You don't want to be alone."

Silence passed between them. "But that doesn't make it right for you to hold us here and make us think we can't leave and abuse us, like you do. It's not right. We're not your prisoners. Whatever people did to you, that wasn't us."

Cassaundra picked up the cigarette she had smoked down to a butt. It was still lit. She put it to her lips and inhaled the smoke as tears streamed down her face.

"Get yo shit and get the fuck out my house."

Wanda stepped back and studied the woman's eyes. "I love you. If no one has ever told you so, I do. I love you, Cassaundra."

"I said, get yo shit! Now!"

The thunder from Cassaundra's words shook the floor again. And rage showed in the woman's eyes as her entire body shook. Wanda shook her head. She felt sorry for the woman. She turned around to walk the halls once more. She walked until she reached the bedroom that had been hers for so long. She remembered standing in front of the door, her little bags in her arms, eyes puffy and red from crying for her daddy. Then she remembered standing there, holding Abby's hand, her eyes puffy from crying for her mama and all the other children she helped Cassaundra to raise, while still raising herself. All their eyes puffy from being abandoned, in some way, by their parents. Wanda sighed and turned the knob on the door in front of her. Their clothing was already in black bags. She and Abby were already packed.

CHAPTER NINE

"What? Put you out? Shut up, girl," Rosa said, holding one of Wanda's bags and quietly closing the door with the other hand, so as not to wake the children.

"Yup. And guess what? She not my legal guardian, either."

"What? Girl, shut up!"

Wanda smiled. "Thanks for putting a smile on my face."

"I ain't playing witchu, girl," Rosa said. "What happened? Come in my room, before these nosey ass kids wake up. Girl, they hear everything."

Wanda followed Rosa to her bedroom. Rosa's house was exceptionally clean and comfortable. Her refrigerator was always full. And her babies had everything they needed. She wasn't like her cousins who blew through their money. She took care of her children and very rarely spent anything on herself, except for her bedroom set. You always want better for your children than you had. Rosa was a good mother. Wanda wondered if it was because they didn't have mothers.

Wanda sat next to Rosa on the soft queen-sized bed, plush with thick blankets, decorated with flowers in earth-tone colors of forest greens, teal, and burnt oranges. The kids weren't allowed to sit on her bed. Rosa didn't allow dirty feet and candy to touch her mattress. She had just gotten it out of layaway. She had saved up for months to afford it.

"Wait. Did you give him some? Wait. Don't tell me. I don't wanna know."

"Naw, girl. Lottie the one told me my daddy got my papers."

"Wow. What Miss Cassaundra say? I know she had a fit. Done kicked ya ass out," laughed Rosa.

"Yea. But really Rose, I feel sorry for her."

"I don't."

"She confessed everything. Told me how she ain't got my papers and how..." Wanda's voice trailed off. She still couldn't believe the news about her daddy. She never would have taken him to stoop that low. You never know what kind of pain people are going through, or what they'd resort to, to ease their pain. No wonder she had such sympathy for Lavenia. The universe must have tried to tell her something.

"Girl, what?" Rosa asked, her voice low.

"Daddy was strung out. That's why he left me. He was on drugs, and Cassaundra ain't want him getting her girls hooked. So she put him out."

"I'm so sorry, girl," said Rosa, touching Wanda's arm. "You know, I know."

"It's okay," Wanda nodded.

"No Wanda, it's not. I keep telling you, you ain't gotta pretend with me. Why you think he did it though?"

"I don't know. The only thing I can think of is the divorce. Must have hit him hard."

"I'll say." Rosa shook her head.

"I do need to stay here a while though, just 'till I get my apartment, me and Abby. I hate to be a burden on you."

"Burden? Girl, bye. I been waiting for this."

The women laughed. But their joy was interrupted by a loud thump that came from the front door.

"The hell?" Rosa stood, and so did Wanda.

The noise thundered again. One of the children started to cry.

"Mommy?" asked a voice.

"Girl, who is knocking your door down like that?"

"I don't know. But they done woke my damn kids. Hold on."

The women walked out of the room. And Rosa stopped to scoop the youngest boy into her arms. Another thump came as she approached the door.

"Hold on one goddamn minute! You gonna knock my door down."

"I don't give a damn. Where she at?" asked the voice.

Rosa stopped and spun around to face Wanda, terror in her face.

"It's Miss Cassaundra."

CHAPTER TEN

Rosa couldn't get the door open wide enough before Cassaundra forced her way in, wobbling through the door frame. Lottie followed behind her. Terror washed over Wanda's face. She had never known Miss Cassaundra to move from her couch too often.

"Where she at?" she thundered, her chest heaving in and out.

"Where who at?" asked Rosa. Wanda was standing right there.

Cassaundra looked Rosa up and down and scowled.

"She *know* what the fuck I'm talking about," Cassaundra said, tilting her head in Wanda's direction. "Where's Abby?"

Wanda stepped back, purposely trying to step in view of the hallway where the children's rooms were.

"Don't be all quiet now. Where is she?"

"But...you...you told us to leave. You put us out," said Wanda, as she trembled, noticeably.

"I put *you* out. I ain't say nothing about that girl. Now *you* can do whatever the fuck you wanna do. But that girl stays here."

This is about money. It's always about money. Losing Abby means she could no longer collect the money. She may not have custody over me. But she could very well be Abby's legal guardian. Wanda thought about her first day there. *"Gone make the call,"* Cassaundra had told Lavenia.

Cassaundra wiggled out of the doorway and stepped back onto the porch, making room for Lottie, who was behind her, to step up and enter the trailer.

"I ain't asking again," she said as Lottie walked into Rosa's living room.

"No," said Wanda.

"Oh, that's what you wanna do? You wanna play games?" asked Cassaundra.

"Wanda..." began Rosa, holding her son.

"No Rose. I can't." This was a fight that needed to happen, that had been building up for years. Rosa's face flushed with concern as she held her baby in her arms.

Lottie grabbed Wanda's arm.

"Now wait one goddamn minute," said Rosa. She put her son down and grabbed Lottie's free arm.

"Rose no," pleaded Wanda. But it was too late. Lottie had pushed Rosa to the side and she fell. He let Wanda's arm go and started toward the back room. Rosa jumped up and raced after him. Wanda ran ahead of Lottie and jumped in front of him. Rosa ran ahead of them of both and disappeared into one of the rooms.

"Move yo ass out the way," said Lottie.

"Do what he says, girl," yelled Cassaundra from the porch. Rosa's door was wide open. Wanda hated that the whole community was going to be in their business. People were probably already exiting their homes and making their way down the road.

"I can't let you do this," said Wanda, looking into Lottie's eyes but talking to Cassaundra. She controlled him like a puppet. Wanda wondered what she had on him.

Lottie grabbed Wanda's shoulders and shoved her to the floor as the cries of Rosa's children soared in from the back room.

"What's going on Miss Williams?" said the voice of

someone nearby. *Here we go*, thought Wanda. The neighbors had made it. There was probably a large crowd outside the door. She couldn't worry about that now though. She had to save Abby. The same way Lavenia had saved her years ago from her mother's abusive man.

"This damn girl always causing some kinda trouble," said Cassaundra's voice.

Lottie pushed past Wanda. And Wanda jumped on his back as he made his way to the back room. He turned around and slammed her back into the wall.

"Ahh!" the cry escaped her lips, louder than she'd wanted it to. She didn't want Lottie to know he could hurt her. Wanda placed her hand on her throbbing lower back. *Shit.*

"Bring both they asses out, Lottie," said Cassaundra's voice.

"You don't have to do this, Miss Williams," someone said.

Wanda struggled to stand. She stumbled over to the room where the children were sleeping. Lottie stood there, stupidly. Wanda smiled. Only Rosa's children were there, huddled up and crying. Rosa and Abby were gone.

"Where they at?" yelled Lottie.

"I don't know," said Wanda, smirking.

Lottie grabbed Wanda's arm and twisted it. "Ahh!" she cried.

"Told you about playing damn games," he twisted her arm some more and forced her to walk toward the front door.

"Where they at?" Cassaundra's face washed with disappointment as Lottie continued to twist Wanda's arm behind her back. Cassaundra wobbled down the steps and looked around the yard. And Lottie walked out of the house and onto the porch, with Wanda's arm still connected to his hand. She winced at the pain as she looked around the yard. *Yup. Everyone out alright. It's gonna be some good gossip about me later.* A cough resounded from the side of the house and Wanda put her head down. *Shit.*

"Lottie! Lottie over here!" yelled Cassaundra, pointing to the side of the trailer as though she was about to win a grand prize.

Wanda thought she heard sirens in the distance, but figured it was hallucination from the pain in her arm.

At Cassaundra's voice, Lottie let Wanda go and raced down the steps and behind the trailer. Wanda held onto her arm.

"Yea. Get her ass," said Cassaundra, wobbling over to the middle of the yard.

Wanda ran after Lottie as best she could, the pain still in her back and arm. She watched in horror as Lottie pulled Rosa and Abby from their hiding place.

"Get yo damn hands offa me," said Rosa.

"Let them go!" screamed Wanda, limping toward them.

"Ya raise 'em up in the way they should go. And this how they treat ya," said Cassaundra, talking to no one in particular. The astonished faces of the neighbors looked on, shaking their heads, in disgust.

"Please. Stop this," cried Wanda.

"Ow!" yelled Lottie. Abby had bit his arm and the shock caused him to release her and Rosa. In the distraction, Abby ran toward Wanda. And Rosa ran into her wide-open front door. She needed to get to her children. Lottie started after her.

"Fuck her," said Cassaundra, waving her hand. "Get Abby, Dumbass!"

Wanda held onto Abby tightly. And the little girl cried as Lottie tried prying them apart.

Sirens.

Again? I'm not tripping, thought Wanda as police cars came into view, disturbing the country roads. Lottie jumped back and Cassaundra stood still. She was too big to make any sudden movements without getting caught so she just stood there, looking dumbfounded.

CHAPTER ELEVEN

"Ma'am? Is this true?"

Two black male police officers stood in the middle of the road. Their cars blocked the entrance as their red and blue lights bounced off the trailers, the dirt road and the faces of the people watching. They said they were responding to a call about a violent disturbance. Rosa, with all five of her children in front of her, had just explained how Lottie and Cassaundra had broken into her home. The officer addressed Cassaundra.

"We ain't break in shit."

The officer held up a hand. "Ma'am."

"Okay. But we ain't break in, is what I'm telling you. She let us in. I was just looking for my daughter," said Cassaundra.

Wanda's jaw clenched as she held onto Abby.

"Did you let them into your home, Ma'am?" The officer addressed Rosa. *That slick witch*, thought Wanda. There was no forced entry or any sign of a forced entry. Rosa had opened the door willingly. She had to tell the truth. Wanda saw Rosa's mouth. "Ain't this a bitch," she mouthed. She knew it too.

"Yes Officer, it's true," Rosa said, frowning.

The other officer shook his head.

"Okay. Well, we're done here, folks. Give the woman back her daughter and ya'll folks have a lovely day," said the officer as both men turned toward their vehicle.

"Thank you, Officer," said Cassaundra.

"Wait!" yelled Wanda. "She's not her daughter."

The officers turned back around, noticeably annoyed.

"Who's not whose daughter, Ma'am?" asked the first officer, the one who looked the most annoyed. He didn't wait for a response. "Can you identify which of these kids belongs to you?" he asked Cassaundra.

"Certainly, Officer," said Cassaundra.

Wanda turned up her lip. *Phony ass.*

"It's that one right there. The one being held hostage," she said, pointing to Abby.

Hostage?

"No. She's lying," said Wanda.

The second officer's shoulders slumped. "Keep this up, and everyone's going to jail."

"We're the hostages, Officer. She's holding us against our will and getting money for it. She's not really our mother."

The officer's eyes got big at Wanda's outburst. But Cassaundra brushed it off with a nervous laugh.

"Officer, I just wanna take my daughter home."

"Do you get money for these children?" asked the officer. Cassaundra's face grew pale.

"She's lying. I got my own money."

The first officer turned his attention to Wanda.

"Those are some pretty serious accusations, young lady."

Cassaundra looked up to the sky and shook her head. Rosa had walked back to her trailer and was sitting on the porch with her children as Wanda held on tightly to Abby.

"Do you have any proof of illegal activity?"

Wanda's heart dropped. Cassaundra had no papers on her. She cut her eyes at the woman and sure enough, there was an evil smirk on her face.

"No physical proof sir," murmured Wanda.

"Any witnesses?"

Wanda sighed. No one was going to tell on Miss Cassaundra around here. She looked around at the crowd.

"No sir. No witnesses."

"Then, there's nothing we can do."

The officers turned toward their vehicle to leave again as a tear rolled down Wanda's cheek. It was over. Cassaundra had won.

The first officer looked at the second officer and then around to everyone still standing on the lawn.

"Alright people. We're done here."

"Wait."

The voice was Lottie's. Wanda had forgotten he was even standing there. "I'm a witness."

Wanda and Rosa's mouth dropped open as Cassaundra's stare tried to burn a hole into Lottie's face. The second officer took out a pen and pad.

"And what's your name?"

"A witness to what?" interrupted the first officer.

Come on man, thought Wanda.

"I know she ain't..." Lottie's voice trailed off as he avoided eye contact with Cassaundra.

"I know she ain't they mama. She never legally adopted them. And I know she been holding them here against they will."

The second officer was writing.

"Your name sir?"

"Oh, uh, Lawrence Williams. Everybody call me Lottie."

What? Wanda's brow buried into her forehead. *Williams?*

"Okay. And do you have proof of these accusations?" asked the second officer.

"These very serious accusations," said the first officer, sarcastically.

Wanda rolled her eyes. She could tell he'd been through this a million times in the hood. He probably wanted to hurry back home to his big brick house in the suburbs and eat his big fancy meal, prepared by his perfect wife.

"Yes, yes sir," Lottie replied.

"Officer..." began Cassaundra.

"Miss, please. Let us do our jobs," said the first officer.

"But he's lyi—"

"You wanna get arrested tonight, Ma'am?"

"No sir," said Cassaundra. Wanda wore the smirk now.

"Would you be willing to come down to the station?"

Lottie cut his eyes at Cassaundra and could feel the heat from her anger across the lawn. He was still standing on the side of the house where he'd grabbed the girls, away from everyone else in the middle of the yard.

"Yes, sir."

"How do we know you're not just covering for them?" asked the first officer, nodding toward Wanda and Rosa.

"Because. I'm her son, sir."

What?

"Oh, hell yes," said Rosa.

Wanda looked behind her, her eyes questioning her friend. *What is happening?*

Rosa smiled and shrugged.

"You're," began the first officer "her son?" he asked, pointing to Miss Cassaundra.

"Yes, sir."

"You're saying, that your mother," began the second officer, the one writing, "kept these kids against their will?"

Lottie looked up for the first time. "Yea."

"And that she's been getting money for them from the government?"

"Yea."

"And that she's been getting this money illegally?"

"Yes," said Lottie again, his face stressed.

"And that you have proof of this?" asked the first officer.

"Yes."

"He's lying!" yelled Cassaundra. She didn't care about being polite. Her real self was beginning to show.

The officers stopped their investigation of Lottie and turned to Wanda.

"How old are you?"

"Sixteen. I'm sixteen."

"How long have you been staying with Miss Cassaundra?"

Wanda looked down and then back up at the officer. "Ten years."

"So, since you were six then?" he asked, writing on a pen and pad.

"Yes, sir."

The officer bent down so that he was face to face with Abby.

"And how old are you?"

Abby remained silent.

"Go on Abby. Tell him," said Wanda. The day's events must have been a lot for her. She had gone back into her shell. But this was not the time to be quiet. The girl looked up at Wanda. "Go on," she reassured her.

"Seven...seven," stammered Abby.

"And what is your name?"

"Abigail Johnson."

"Thank you," said the officer. "You're very brave."

The man stood. "If your parents are still alive, we have to notify them and investigate to prove these claims. If what you people say is true, then she's..." the officer nodded toward Cassaundra. Cassaundra rolled her eyes. "...not the only one in trouble here. Why didn't your parents look for you? Or file a missing person's report?"

Wanda looked down again. She had no idea where her parents were. Snitching on Miss Cassaundra had backfired. She hadn't meant for everyone to get in trouble.

"I believe you. But there are a lot of loose ends. Are you sure you want to go down this road? It won't be easy."

Wanda lifted her head and met Lottie's eyes. He nodded. She turned to face Cassaundra's scowl.

"Yes Officer. I'm sure."

"We have to bring you all down to the station," said the first officer. "Yes, that means you too," he said, pointing to the porch where Rosa and her children sat. Rosa rolled her eyes.

The first officer approached Cassaundra.

"Turn around for me please, Ma'am."

"Officer. Officer please. Listen to me. They lying. All they asses is lying!" she screamed as the officer reached out and grabbed both her hands, twisting them behind her back. The neighbors looked on, whispering among themselves.

"Ow! You hurting me. This is harassment!" yelled Cassaundra.

"Cassaundra Williams, you are under arrest for fraud and kidnapping...."

"Lies! All Lies! Everything I've done for you, and this is what I get?" Cassaundra was hysterical as the officers led her to the vehicle.

"You have the right to remain silent. Anything you say can and will be used against you in a court of law...."

"I took you in. Put clothes on your back, food in your stomach, and this the thanks I get?" Cassaundra addressed Wanda as the first officer stuffed her body into the vehicle. But it didn't help. She continued to shout out the open window.

"Ma'am. Please be silent. Anything you say can and will be used against you in the court of law," said the second officer.

"I don't care. Her ass is lying! I'm the only one ever been there for you! When ya mama and daddy left ya, who was there? Me. I was. I was there!" she yelled as tears rolled down Wanda's eyes.

"You have the right to an attorney. If you cannot afford an attorney, one will be provided for you. Do you understand the rights I have just read to you? With these rights in mind, do you wish to speak to me?"

"Fuck you. Fuck them. Fuck ya'll," cursed Cassaundra from the back seat.

CHAPTER TWELVE

After the cops took Cassaundra, they said they would be back for everyone else involved. Rosa had begged them to let her get her children ready. This was also to help to buy them some down time, a small break before more drama began. The children needed it. The officers would send for them in an hour.

People walked up to Wanda to offer their apologies and testimonies on how wrong they knew Cassaundra was. Stories came out about how she'd abused Lottie since he was a boy and how she had used him to manipulate girls and women. Wanda rolled her eyes. *Why do black people wait until it's too late to admit they knew someone or something was wrong? I suffered for years and now you tell me you knew? Why didn't you say something then?*

But Wanda kept quiet and fake smiled through their stories, her arms around Abby. If it wasn't for this little girl, the truth would have probably never come out. She would have left Cassaundra's house and moved on with her life. But then, there would have been some other little girl to replace her. Or she could have let Cassaundra take Abby and moved on with her life. Instead, she fought. Maybe it was because she was still a little girl, a trapped little girl, waiting to be rescued. Sometimes life matures you in a way that makes you forget how young you really are. Maybe that's why Abby's screams awoke the fight in her. A fight she was still fighting. But for once, it looked like she would win.

Wanda waved to the last of the neighbors and walked with

Abby up Rosa's steps, through the front door and into the living room, closing the door behind them.

"Finally, some damn privacy," said Rosa when Wanda closed the door. Both women sat on the couch.

"You okay, Baby?" Rosa asked Abby. Abby shook her head.

"Why don't you go on in the back with the kids," said Wanda.

"Yea and tell them to hurry up," said Rosa. "Ya'll come on!" she yelled.

You just told them for her. Wanda shook her head, watching as Abby ran in the back. She picked up a toy ball sitting in front of them and tossed it around.

"Ain't this some shit?" laughed Rosa. "The drama!"

The women laughed.

"It is crazy," agreed Wanda.

"It makes sense though. That's why it was so easy for her to boss him around," said Rosa.

"Yea, ole *Lawrence*," said Wanda, mockingly. The friends laughed. "Why you think he do it Rose? Why he take up for me like that?"

"Girl, he probably tired of her ass. I know I would be tired of somebody bossing my ass around."

"I think he planned it," said Wanda.

"What you mean?"

"I mean, why would he tell me Miss Cassaundra ain't got my papers? I know this is gonna sound weird. But it's like he saved me, in a way."

"Damn, that's deep, Sis."

There was silence for a moment as the women were each in their own thoughts until someone knocked on the door.

"No. Go away!" yelled Rosa as Wanda laughed and answered the door. Lavenia stood in front of her.

"Hey Miss L. What are you doing here?"

Wanda opened the door wider so Lavenia could step in.

"Lavenia? You okay?" asked Rosa, from the couch.

"I just came to check on ya'll," said Lavenia. Wanda's heart melted.

"Aww Miss L. We okay."

"Yea, thanks for checking up on us," said Rosa. "You need some money?"

Wanda turned around and scowled at Rosa. She knew better than to offer Miss L some money, knowing what she would do with it. Rosa shrugged.

Lavenia shook her head quickly. "No. That's okay, Baby. Thomas is …. Thomas is on his way. I just came to check on ya'll. I heard the policemens came."

"Thomas?" Wanda smirked. Thomas was Brandon's daddy. She folded her arms. "What Thomas doing picking you up?"

"He gonna take Brandon for a while. I'm gonna go ahead and check in."

"Hey!" shouted Rosa, standing.

"Oh Miss L. That's great news!" said Wanda, hugging Lavenia. "You gonna do good too. I know you will."

Lavenia shook her head and Wanda said a silent prayer. She's gonna need all the support she can get. Crack was nothing to play with, and getting over it was not going to be easy. *I guess we all still fighting.*

"Wait," said Rosa. "How you know the police was here?"

Wanda rolled her eyes. "Girl, who don't know the police were here!"

Lavenia smiled as the women went back and forth. Wanda saw her grin.

"Miss L! You called them. Didn't you!"

Lavenia laughed and so did Rosa and Wanda. Turns out Lavenia was the real hero. So far, she had saved Abby twice. This was gonna go down in the history books of most surprises in one day. The women laughed and talked with Lavenia some more before seeing her off. Wanda closed the door behind her.

"Well, you did it," said Rosa.

"Did what?"

"Killed the Wicked Witch of the West."

Wanda laughed, remembering their favorite childhood movie. "We still gotta go to court."

"Ding-dong the witch is dead, the witch is dead, the witch is dead. Ding-dong the wicked witch is dead!" sang Rosa, dancing.

Wanda laughed. "You crazy."

The children came from the back room and joined Rosa on the dance floor, laughing and singing. Wanda watched as Abby danced along with Egypt. It was good to see Abby happy. Wanda curled her lip. *Damn.* She could forget about Mrs. Clark and that apartment. Ain't no way she was gonna make the deadline with court and all this mess. At least they were free from Cassaundra though, and that was a start.

"What the hell," said Wanda, shaking free from her thoughts. May as well enjoy this victory. *Who knows what the next few days will have in store?*

"Ding-dong the witch is dead, the witch is dead, the witch is dead!" she sang. "Ding-dong the wicked witch is dead!"

Thank you for reading my book!

It would mean a great deal to me if you could give me your opinion. Not only will this let me know what you feel about my writing in general, but potential readers will also value your feedback in the form of an Honest Review.

Finally, I would be delighted to hear from you by email at yecheilyah@yecheilyahysrayl.com *about the book.*

Thank you very much for taking the time to let me know your opinion. Best wishes, Yecheilyah Ysrayl.

www.ingramcontent.com/pod-product-compliance
Lightning Source LLC
Chambersburg PA
CBHW082059090726
47909CB00011B/3090